The Hockey Girls

Other books by Scott Corbett

THE BIG JOKE GAME
STEADY, FREDDIE!
TAKE A NUMBER

The Hockey Girls

by Scott Corbett

E. P. Dutton & Co., Inc.   New York

Library of Congress Cataloging in Publication Data

Corbett, Scott   The hockey girls

SUMMARY: The new compulsory sports program throws the
freshman girls at Wagstaff High into a fury, until they
get involved.

[1. Field hockey—Fiction]   I. Title.
PZ7.C79938Hk   [Fic]   75-33804   ISBN 0-525-32065-2

Published simultaneously in Canada by Clarke,
Irwin & Company Limited, Toronto and Vancouver

Designed by Nancy Danahy
Printed in the U.S.A.
10 9 8 7 6 5 4 3 2

To Julie Baldwin with many thanks

1

Irma and Marilee could hardly wait to get to a back seat in the school bus to hold an indignation meeting. If high school was going to be like *this*, then they were ready to become a couple of dropouts!

Irma fired the opening gun.

"I *hate* Mrs. Cranshaw!"

"Mizzzz Cranshaw," Marilee reminded her. Ms. Cranshaw was the new assistant principal at Wagstaff High. Furthermore, she had gotten together with some of the mizzes in the front office over at Hyde Park High and they were going to start the same thing there!

"An athletic program for girls! *Yuk!*" said Irma, pronouncing the word with all the throw-uppy emphasis she could give it.

"Why us? Why do *we* have to be the goats? 'Every girl in the freshman class is to participate in at least one sport,' " said Marilee through her nose, imitating the tone of voice used by Ms. Cranshaw in making the announcement at assembly.

"It's all because she's a big fem-libber! We're lucky she doesn't expect us to play on the football team with the boys!"

"That'll come next," Marilee predicted grimly.

"Well, they're not going to suck *me* into it, and that's that!" Irma would have folded her arms defiantly if they had not already been folded around her schoolbag. "It's too much!"

Gym, of course, was compulsory; they had expected that. But the word from older sisters had always been that the gym program was not very strenuous. But compulsory sports! No prospect could have been worse. Irma's idea of an outdoor sport was reading a book in a hammock.

"Why did I have to be the youngest?" mourned Marilee, thinking of her older sisters. "Meg and Marsha went through four years at Wagstaff and hardly had to turn a hand!"

"Or a handspring," added Irma gloomily, remembering how she had suffered last year in the eighth grade when she had to take gym.

2

Marilee had been more fortunate during her elementary school career.

"What's a handspring?" she asked innocently.

"It's a form of Oriental torture," replied Irma. "The details are too revolting to go into."

They continued to talk in this vein until Mr. Hanson braked to a pig-squeal stop at their corner. And of course as they came up the aisle that classroom comic Gino Minelli had to have something to say. He nudged his pal Sammy Arbuckle.

"Hey, look, here come Chris Evert and Peggy Fleming!"

Irma gave him an icy glare.

"I hope you fumble on the one-yard line," was her crusher, and she left him to go into his tiresome falsetto routine— "Oh, Sammy, did you hear what that nasty girl said to me? I'm gonna cry!"

Mr. Hanson glanced up as he opened the door for them.

"Say, what's eating all you girls today? I never saw such a bunch of wet hens."

Irma sighed.

"We've had some bad news," she told him, sounding as if there had been a death in the family.

He grinned with sudden understanding. "Oh! You mean the new ath-a-letic program? Why, shucks, it'll be the making of you!"

"Sure," said Irma. "It'll make a man out of me."

"I wouldn't worry about that!" retorted Mr. Hanson raffishly, causing both girls to color up a bit. They stepped stiffly off the bus and glared after it as it rumbled away.

"That Mr. Hanson is so *fresh!*" said Irma. "We ought to report him."

"Wouldn't do a bit of good," grumped Marilee.

Fresh or not, Mr. Hanson's observation had been correct. Both girls had already heard a few whistles, especially Marilee, who had developed a womanly figure. Irma had not yet become a slim goddess—she was still a skinny kid—but there was promise.

Marilee Barnes had carroty red hair and some attractive freckles she naturally hated. Irma Tuttle had light brown hair that always raised her hopes by bleaching out in a blondish direction under the summer sun and then dashed them by returning to brown with indecent haste about one day after Labor Day.

The corner of Sea and South streets, where the bus stopped, was where they parted. Irma went one way down South Street, Marilee the other. Today, of course, they lingered for a moment, getting off a few final squawks.

"And the *choice* they're offering!" said Marilee, brooding over the list of sports Ms. Cranshaw had unveiled. "Did you ever hear anything so *unappetizing* in your life?"

"If only we got more snow and had some decent hills around here!" said Irma, surveying their gently rolling countryside with dissatisfied eyes. "If only we did, I'd go out for tobogganing. At least you can do that sitting down."

"Or sailing," said Marilee, dreaming of summertime and no school. "At least we both like to sail."

They collaborated on heavy sighs.

"Well, we'll just have to think of some way out," said Irma, and on that note they parted.

Ordinarily Irma Tuttle was happy with her surroundings, living as she did in a village encircled by woods and fields, where there was plenty of room to move around in—at her own pace. But right now she was not so sure. She was willing to bet most city kids did not have to go through anything like *this* and be threatened with an athletics program by some busybody like Ms. Cranshaw. As she trudged homeward along the pleasant, winding, tree-lined road, Irma was in no mood to count her blessings.

Up ahead of her the two crab-apple trees on the left-hand side had been having a busy day. Dozens of the small apples had fallen on the road, and only a few of them had been squashed by the tires of the occasional car that traveled it.

She stopped, put her schoolbag down on the bank, and scrambled up to get her stick. Speaking of moods, she was just in the mood to work off some of her steam by whacking a few crab apples.

Her stick was one she always left leaning against the same maple tree. Winter and summer it had been there for two years now. She had seen it sticking up out of a snowdrift, she had seen it glistening with cold spring rains, patiently waiting for the advent of the next crab-apple season. It was an old friend, Old Faithful. She had found it one day by the side of the road, a fairly straight branch with a twist at the end that made it just right for whacking crab apples. All its bark had gradually peeled off until now it was as smooth and yellow-white as old ivory.

Returning to the road, she squared off and took three shots at the telephone pole, hitting it with two out of three crab apples. Next, after selecting a special apple with an eye to size and roundness, she began running it up the road. She liked to see if she could guide one through all the other crab apples without touching them, all the way from the maple tree to the telephone pole, and then finish off by whacking it between the two little willows a few yards past the telephone pole.

As she fooled around with Old Faithful her mind was busy with this newest threat to her existence. Athletics program! The very words sounded hot and sweaty. Day after day of getting dressed in a steamy locker room and then slaving through a lot of dreary exercise until her face was red and her hair was stringy, and thinking the whole time about all the pleasant things she might otherwise be doing on her own—why, she would feel just like poor old Tantalus, up to her neck in misery, with the good things of life out of reach! (They were studying mythology in Miss Tingley's English class, and had heard all about Tantalus's uncomfortable situation in Hades. To put it in terms of still another story from mythology, she felt like that fellow trying to get out of the Labyrinth. There had to be a way out.)

After casting about in her mind for a while in search of ideas, she suddenly called a time-out and clutched the front of her blouse somewhat dramatically.

What about her heart?

Now, there was a thought. Would it be good for a growing girl to strain herself when she had a *systolic murmur of the apex* . . . she couldn't remember the rest of it, but there *was* something about her heart. . . . Yes, but she couldn't depend on it, or on Doctor Ben, darn him! No, she needed something more than that. . . .

Then a lovely idea blossomed in her mind like a white rose.

Her knee!

Dropping Old Faithful, she yanked up the left leg of her blue jeans until her knee came into sight. Kneeling on her right knee, she examined the left one intently.

Either she had the wrong knee, or the scar had disappeared. She switched her position to check her right knee.

Yes!

The scar was still there, and even as she looked at it she could feel her knee begin to ache in a most satisfying way. How could she have forgotten it was her right knee?

Her poor, damaged knee! Who was to say it might not give way at any moment? She could not claim to have a football knee—but what was wrong with a hopscotch knee? She could still remember how she had fallen and given that knee such a terrible bang when she was playing hopscotch that time with Elsie Macdougal. All that blood, and she'd had to have three stitches!

Back to his tree went Old Faithful; there was no more time for crab apples today. Grabbing her schoolbag, she hurried on home as fast as she could without actually running—with that knee, after all, she had no business actually running.

She would be lucky if she could even ride her bicycle as far as Doctor Ben's!

2 _____

"I'm going to ride around, Mom. Maybe over to Marilee's."

"All right, dear. Don't be late for supper."

She had said nothing as yet at home about the new athletics program. Her parents would have to be a last resort. She had to handle this whole tricky problem very carefully, or she might blow it. The chances of getting a note out of *them* asking the school to excuse her from athletics was about nil, she well knew.

Even if she promised to do all sorts of extra chores and keep her room neat and never go around with any boys they didn't like and heaven knew what else, she was not likely to get anywhere. Even the business of appealing to their old family doctor was better done on her own, before they knew anything about it.

While she was getting her bike out of the garage her mother appeared at the back door and waved a piece of paper.

"As long as you're going over to Marilee's, take this pattern back to Mrs. Dixon for me, will you, Irma?"

"Sure, Mom."

Irma was eager to make tracks for Doctor Ben's, but she did not want to stir up any question-and-answer periods by looking as if she were in a big hurry to go somewhere. She took the dress pattern and put it in her pocket without further comment. Still, it was annoying. Now she would not only have to go out of her way, but way out of her way to go *out of* her way, so to speak—because Mrs. Dixon lived on South Street a few doors the other side of Marilee's house, and Irma did not want Marilee to see her riding around and maybe decide to join her.

So that meant Irma had to ride around the block—up Sea Street, across Beeman, and down Fillmore—and turn into South Street again from the other end. All that took time, and then of course Mrs. Dixon had to talk for a while—she was a great talker—and after that Irma had to go back around the block again the way she had come. Why was it that every time you wanted to do anything the least bit secret, everything got so complicated?

At last, however, she was back on Sea Street and pedaling toward the road that would take her to her self-made doctor's appointment. Doctor Ben Fulton lived a couple of miles away, not far from the next village.

The mailbox labeled "Fulton" stood in front of a handsome, rambling old clapboard house with three or four chimneys and a general air of having been around for a long, long time—like Doctor Fulton, for that matter. He was supposed to be retired, except that people wouldn't let him be, and he could not resist continuing to take care of a few of his old patients. He always said the only reason he was willing to keep Irma and her parents on his list was because none of them ever got sick.

During her more pessimistic moments while bicycling over, she had decided it would be just her luck not to find him at home. But she was wrong. She did not even have to undergo the suspense of ringing his doorbell. He was out in his side yard in old clothes, weeding a bed of his famous chrysanthemums, whistling while he worked, obviously in a good mood.

In a wild swing toward sunny optimism, Irma could not help feeling that all omens were good.

Doctor Ben Fulton looked a lot like Santa Claus might look if he shaved. Using his own figure as a bad example, he had always been a tyrant about his patients' diets. But as Irma came walking across the yard toward him—limping slightly, it seemed—he looked at her lead-pencil build approvingly. No extra lard there.

"Hi, Irma. What's the matter, did you twist your ankle?"

Irma smiled bravely, with a smile that did its best (while failing, of course) to conceal the pain that lay behind it.

"No, it's my knee, Doctor Ben. The one I fell on that time."

"Oh?" The good doctor racked his brain for a moment, wondering what on earth she was talking about, and finally recalled the incident. "Oh, yes, I remember. Had to have a couple of stitches, didn't you?"

"Three!"

"Three, was it? How old were you then, Irma?"

"Well, about eight, I guess."

"And you mean to say it's troubling you now?"

Irma shrugged.

"A little," she admitted.

"Hmm. Let me see it."

Carefully Irma hitched up the leg of her blue jeans—the right one; how could she ever have forgotten it?—baring the old wound. Squatting down, Doctor Ben peered at it and touched the kneecap gently here and there with fingertips steeped in the ancient art of healing.

"Hmm." He straightened up and shook his

head in a grave way. "I think we'd better go inside for a more thorough examination," he said, causing Irma's heart to bound joyfully and thump apprehensively at almost the same instant. Maybe it was worse than she thought, maybe there really *was* something wrong with her knee! Oh, but how could that be? No, there could hardly be much wrong—but maybe just enough to do the job!

Doctor Ben glanced at his watch and added, "But before we go in I've got to step down to the orchard for a minute to check up on a couple of my beehives. You're not afraid of bees, I hope?"

"No!" sang Irma. In her present hopeful mood she was ready to face lions, if necessary—and anyway, she really wasn't afraid of bees, having been around beehives before at her Uncle Matt's place.

"Good. Then how about walking down with me? That'll give me a chance to see how much that knee seems to be troubling you, and that'll help me when it comes to the examination."

"Sure!" said Irma, and fell into step beside him, remembering to limp just the tiniest bit, without overdoing it.

"Ever seen my apple orchard, Irma?"

Irma said she hadn't.

"Well, then, it's high time you paid it a visit. It's one of the finest orchards in the state, if I do say so myself."

On the way down the hill Doctor Ben explained that although the apples were already forming up nicely on the trees, they would not be ready to eat until after the first frost, a month or so from now, because it took a frost to bring out their flavor. Irma did her best to look interested and listen politely, but she scarcely heard him, she was so busy thinking happy thoughts about hitting the jackpot. Wait till Marilee saw her note from Doctor Ben! Would she be jealous!

The sight of the orchard ahead of them, with its apples reddening everywhere amid the green of the leaves, did make her forget herself for a while.

"Oh, that's *beautiful!*" she said, delighting Doctor Ben.

"Just for that I'll bring you some, round about Halloween time," he said.

They walked into the orchard between two rows of trees, and Irma was moved to cry, "Why, it's a regular Paradise!"

Then all at once the orchard began to resemble Paradise in one of its unhappier moments, and Irma suddenly experienced something of what Mother Eve had been up against there. Sliding down the trunk of an apple tree came a huge black snake, its skin glittering like sooty chain mail.

While Irma's footsteps faltered to a quick stop, the great snake slithered across the open space ahead of them on a diagonal and slipped up the trunk of another tree farther on. Doctor Ben, still busy talking about apples, did not seem to notice. But then he realized she had stopped, and he glanced back at her.

"What's the matter, Irma?"

She was too frightened to do more than point—because now another enormous black snake, and another, and another, had come down from trees on both sides and were crisscrossing the open space. Doctor Ben turned to see what she was looking at with such terrified eyes, and let out a yell.

"Good grief, we've walked into a *nest* of them! Get going, Irma—I'll hold them off!"

Afterwards she could not even remember how she got back to the house. All she knew was that a very short time later she was inside, slamming the back door behind her.

Meanwhile, down in the orchard, Doctor Ben was casting a mild eye around him.

"Thanks, fellows," he said, "I knew I could count on you."

Standing at a window a couple of minutes later, Irma heaved a sigh of relief and stopped debating with herself about whether or not she should call the police, now that she had her breath back. She knew black snakes were not poisonous, of course, but when there were that many of them, and such big ones, there was no telling what they might be able to do! She remembered that picture of Laocoön being strangled by great serpents—another of Miss Tingley's goodies from mythology—and was vastly relieved when Doctor Ben came in sight and appeared to be all right. And since no serpents seemed to be pursuing him, she even got up nerve enough to go to the door and step out onto the back porch.

"Are you all right, Doctor Ben?"

"Safe and sound," he assured her. He stumped up onto the porch and said, "Let's go inside."

She followed him, waiting for further comments on their narrow escape, but he simply marched through the house to his examining room and picked up a stethoscope.

"Let's have a listen."

He put the end of it against her chest and adjusted the earpieces in his ears. Irma's spirits soared again. After an experience like that her heart would probably be in the last stages of disrepair. She would not even need to depend on her knee now!

Doctor Ben listened. Then he put the stethoscope aside.

"Sound as a bell," he said. "You know, that heart murmur of yours isn't even a defect, anyway, it's simply a harmless little variation on the run-of-the-mill."

While that sound heart of hers was sinking like a stone in a pond, Doctor Ben cleared up a few matters.

"Irma Tuttle, you can run like a jackrabbit.

You went up that hill like greased lightning. And the truth is, those blackies down there are the nicest, tamest bunch of farmer's helpers you ever saw. I've always encouraged them, because they help keep the orchard clear of mice and rats and other varmints, and they've never been known to eat an apple. That running back and forth they do is just their way of showing they're glad to see me—they do it every time I go down there. Why, I wouldn't take a hundred dollars for one of those fellows!"

Irma sat down hard on a chair, blank-faced with indignation.

"Doctor Ben! You're a—a—"

"I sure am!" he agreed with a nasty chuckle, "and do you know what you are, Irma? You're the third girl that's been here to see me since school got out. Dodie Fenwick made it here first, and Marilee Barnes came in second."

"*Marilee!*" Irma bounced in fury on her chair. "Why, that *sneak!* She didn't even tell me she was planning to—"

"If you ask me, you ought to go out for track, Irma. Why, you must have made that hundred-yard dash in about eight seconds—and uphill at that! I was only sorry I didn't have my stopwatch with me," said Doctor Ben, continuing to revel in his mean enjoyment.

"So!" Irma glowered at him. "You know about the new athletics program!"

"I do now," said Doctor Ben. "Well, they say

misery loves company, so you'll be glad to know that neither the broken collarbone Dodie claims never mended properly nor the terrible back-aches that keep Marilee awake night after night are going to interfere with their athletic careers."

"*Back*aches? Why, Marilee Barnes never had a backache in her life! She's as limber as a—as a snake!"

"Okay, well, now you run along before I have to give you a bill, and don't let me hear anything more about that knee. Just go out there and win for dear old Wagstaff High!" urged Doctor Ben, and had himself another good laugh which Irma did not join in on.

3_____

There were some sharp exchanges when best friends met at the bus stop next morning.

"Marilee Barnes, that was sneaky of you not to tell me you were going over to Doctor Ben's!"

"Who told you I went?"

"Doctor Ben!"

"Oh! So you went over, too—and you never told me *you* were going!"

"I didn't think of it till I was walking home!"

"Well, neither did I!"

So that was a standoff, and after a few lesser exchanges they decided to forgive and forget. Irma told Marilee what Doctor Ben had done to her, and Marilee decided that she herself had gotten off easily after all.

"Why? What did he do to you, Marilee?"

"Well, I got Buddy to drive me over"—Buddy was her older brother—"and Doctor Ben was weeding a flower bed—"

"He still was when I came."

"—so I went over to him, walking kind of slow, and told him about my backaches. He said, 'Well, we'd better go in so I can examine you. Help me gather up these tools and we'll go,' and like a fool I started picking up trowels and things, and all at once while I was bending over he gave me this terrific smack on the bottom and said, '*I'll* give you a backache, all right! Now, get back in that car and I don't want to hear anything more from you till I read in the papers about how you won the hundred-yard backstroke for dear old Wagstaff!' Dodie Fenwick had already been there and he knew all about the new program!"

"That Dodie! How did she ever move fast enough to get there first?"

"Listen, she can move when she has to—and she probably figured she *had* to protect her eye makeup!"

Irma nodded, and indicated by a hopeless slump of her shoulders the tragic course her own story was about to follow.

"Well, after Doctor Ben I just gave up," she declared. "Oh, I made a try at home, of course—I told them about Ms. Cranshaw's terrible ideas and how I hated the whole thing and couldn't see why I should have to take athletics if I didn't want to, and how it would cut into my study time and probably ruin my marks—"

"Bilge. I said the same things, though," admitted Marilee. "I did my best to work up a good case of hysterics, even, but I couldn't really throw myself into it, because I knew it was hopeless."

"Of course. But don't you love the way *they* sit there looking smug and talking about how it will do us a lot of good when you know darn well neither one of our mothers ever had to play anything when they were in high school? And Daddy! When I finally told them about Doctor Ben he almost fell out of his chair laughing. He's a real sympathetic type, a regular TV daddy, that one!"

For a moment they brooded silently on the unfairness of it all.

"Well, outside of breaking a leg I just don't see any way of getting excused," said Marilee.

"Neither do I," said Irma. "We're simply going to have to think of something else."

For a moment, on their way to Miss Tingley's first-period English class, their hopes were raised by Bunky Bergman.

"How can we have all those teams without coaches, and where is Ms. Cranshaw going to find that many coaches?" she demanded to know. "Don't worry, her old program will never get off the ground!"

But Fran Sealey, always a wet blanket, was right there to put a damper on this comforting prognosis.

"Don't kid yourself," she said from between those tight lips of hers, "Ms. Cranshaw is a real ball of fire. She's already got volunteers lined up—parents and other people—and some of the teachers are even going to help."

This news was received with groans and resentful looks. Fran Sealey was even suspected of secretly admiring Ms. Cranshaw, when it came to that. And she did not help matters now with her disdainful reaction to their disapproval.

"Well, I don't care, *I'm* looking forward to having a decent sports program, because *I* believe in keeping fit even though the rest of you don't," she said with a darting glance that maliciously probed various local areas of baby fat, and added a final zinger, knowing full well the response she would get. "Besides, we'll only be having practice three times a week."

"*Only* three?" At least four voices joined in on that group groan, but Fran was already walking off in her straight-backed way, leaving mutterers behind. She was a great one for always walking with perfect posture and holding her head high.

"She thinks she's so good!" said one mutterer.

"She *is* good," snapped Irma. "That's what's so bad about her!"

Irma was remembering Fran in their eighth-grade gym class, doing all that stuff on the parallel bars and loving it.

"She'll be another Ms. Cranshaw when she grows up," somebody predicted gloomily.

"Then I feel sorry for our kids!" said Irma.

All sorts of rumors were flying, but at the end of her second-period history class Irma overheard one she could believe, a rumor that Mr. Gluck was going to coach swimming.

The timing was good, because she had him for math third period. Not only that, but the instant she heard the rumor a brilliant idea hit her. She rushed down the hall to Mr. Gluck's room ahead of everyone else, as fast as her hopscotch knee would carry her.

Why hadn't she thought of it before? Every team would have to have a manager! She was one of Mr. Gluck's best math students—he *knew* she had organizing ability and could keep track of things—she was even sort of a favorite of his, she felt pretty sure. . . .

Mr. Gluck listened to her request with a poker face that was worse than being laughed at.

"I'll have to put you on standby, Irma," he said. "You're the fifteenth girl, or maybe it's the sixteenth, who's hit me for the job. It's tough luck, not getting here till third period. But I'm glad to take your application for the team, because I hear you're the best swimmer over on your side of the township."

"*Me?*" Irma's voice went squeaky with alarm. "Why, I'm not even a good dog-paddler! You must have me confused with Marilee! She can swim rings around me!"

The instant the words were out of her mouth she felt like a rat fink, but then it was too late. Mr. Gluck was looking interested.

"Marilee, eh? I'm glad you told me, I'll grab her for the team," he said, making a note on his pad. "I'll put you down as a possibility, too, in case all your managerial prospects fall through."

At that point Irma was very glad that Marilee did not have math with Mr. Gluck till last period, after which Marilee would not be riding home on the bus because her mother was picking her up for a dentist appointment.

The crab-apple trees had been generous again with their fruit, so Irma stopped for a while to give Old Faithful a workout. Somehow she had gotten this insane feeling that the old stick would have been disappointed if she had let a day of their season go by without whacking a few, and anyway, it was good to relax and get her mind off her troubles for a while.

Not that she was entirely successful. As she flipped apples this way and that, and threaded one through a maze of the others with practiced ease, her mind kept going back in a guilty way to her betrayal of Marilee. But before long, of course, she found excuses for herself. What was so wrong about it, anyway? If they all had to go out for something, why wouldn't Marilee be better off doing something she was good at?

While soothing herself with Old Faithful and the crab apples, Irma was soon able to convince herself she had practically done Marilee a favor and that Marilee would *thank* her for speaking to Mr. Gluck about her, once she got used to the idea. Preoccupied as she was, Irma did not even notice the car parked some fifty yards up the road in a neighbor's driveway until it started up and came toward her. She stepped off the road to let the car pass, but it stopped, and she was surprised to see who was at the wheel. It was her English teacher, Miss Tingley.

Miss Tingley was a small, wiry, white-haired lady about a thousand years old, and reputed by a couple of generations of her former pupils to be the best English teacher in the whole state. She could have had any teaching program she wanted—only seniors, for example—but she always insisted on having one class of freshmen, and Irma knew she was lucky to be in it. Miss Tingley was a grammar nut, a literature nut, a mythology nut—a woman of countless enthusiasms—all of which she communicated with fiery dedication and surprising success to her classes.

At the moment, however, another enthusiasm was on her mind. Beaming out at Irma in her fierce way, she waggled a pair of field glasses at her.

"I've been scouting you, Irma," she said, "and you're just what I'm looking for!"

Irma was bewildered.

"I . . . I am? What for, Miss Tingley?"

"Irma, back in the Devonian Period, or maybe it was the Cambrian, when I was attending a girls' school, I was captain of our undefeated, championship field hockey team. I've always had a high regard for the game—a true character-builder, it is—so I was only too glad to volunteer my services as coach of *our* field hockey team. And you're going to be our star forward! Irma, you're a natural!"

"M-me? What do you mean, Miss Tingley?"

"Well, look at the way you handle that stick! The way you hit those apples toward the exact spot where you want them to go!"

"But, gee, Miss Tingley, I'm not playing on a team in a game. I'm just doing it for *fun!*"

"Well, good heavens, child, playing on a team in a game can be fun, too—and with tremendous satisfaction and a sense of achievement as additional rewards. The windy plains of Troy, the clash of arms, the noble feats of Hector and Achilles—it's all there in miniature! You'll love it, Irma! See me tomorrow morning, and sign up."

4 _____

"Irma Tuttle, I'll never speak to you again!" yelled Marilee, and immediately spoke to her again. "Of all the rotten things to do, going behind my back to Mr. Gluck—"

"Who are *you* to talk?" Irma retorted furiously. "Don't tell me it wasn't *you* that told Miss Tingley about *me!* Who else knows about the crab apples? I was a fool ever to show you my stick and let you play that time—"

"I didn't tell her on purpose, it just slipped out!" cried Marilee. "She grabbed me and told me she was going to coach field hockey and she had her eye on me, and—well, I had to say *some-*

thing, so I said I wasn't a bit good at it, I couldn't even hit a crab apple when I tried once with you. . . ."

"Marilee, you *skunk!*"

"It just slipped out!" she repeated, sticking to her story. "And of course then Miss Tingley got it all out of me. Well, gee, you know you *are* good, and. . . ."

In time, of course, they both had to simmer down and admit they had each let a little something slip out, and no use crying over spilt milk. But even so, Marilee still had to shed a few more verbal tears.

"I didn't even get to *ask* for manager," she groaned. "Mr. Gluck told me I was on the team before I even got my mouth open!"

"Oh—you thought of manager, too, huh?" said Irma in a discouraged tone of voice. But she resolutely put all that in the past and decided it was time to start working Marilee in the direction of that gratitude she was eventually going to feel.

"Well, really, Marilee, I can't see what's so awful about it, anyway," she said, dropping into a shamelessly reasonable and persuasive tone of voice. "You have to go out for something, so why not have it be something that you're really good at?"

"Ha!" Marilee gave her a dark look. "You don't know the half of it. I haven't told you the worst yet. I haven't *begun* to tell you. You think it's just swimming. Well, let me tell you, it's not.

Do you know what that crazy Mr. Gluck has decided on? *With* Ms. Cranshaw's blessing?"

"No. What?"

"Water polo!"

"*Water* polo?"

"Water polo. He says we ought to have a real team sport, so it's going to be water polo. So thanks to *you* I'm going to have to chase a foolish ball all over the swimming pool and have a whole nother team trying to do nothing but drown me!"

Irma was shaken. Marilee's fate was indeed so awful that in self-defense she had to categorize her own hideous prospects.

"Okay, that's not so hot—but how about me? Running my silly legs off, getting my shins clobbered by everybody else's hockey stick, getting bumped off my feet. . . ."

It was a gloomy session they had. To say that they were merely dismayed was like saying that Marsyas was a bit upset when Apollo flayed him alive (that being still another happy little mythology story Miss Tingley had introduced them to). But there was no escape from the windy plains of Troy. Two days later every able-bodied girl in the freshman class had been grabbed by one press-gang or another, and practice was scheduled to begin on the following Monday.

"Kilts?"

When she heard what they were to wear,

Dodie Fenwick was so shocked she stopped buffing her nails.

"That's right," said Irma. "Miss Tingley says we're to wear a kilt or kilt-type skirt, long socks, and sneakers. She says we'll do without rubber-cleated hockey shoes because of the expense."

"But why can't we just wear jeans?"

"Because we have to wear shin guards. We couldn't pull the legs of jeans down over them, and we'd look pretty silly wearing them out-side."

"We're going to look pretty silly no matter *what* we wear—but a kilt! Why, I wouldn't be caught dead in one!"

"Wanna bet?" said Irma, remembering who had given the order. Dodie remembered, too, and reconsidered.

"Well, anyway, I wouldn't wear one to school. I suppose I'll change for practice if I have to. But kilts! Why, we'll look like a bunch of—of *schoolgirls!*"

Irma laughed, delighted with this splendid Dodieism, while Dodie greeted her laughter with her usual puzzled expression.

"What's the matter, Irma?"

"Well, we *are* schoolgirls, aren't we?"

"Oh. Well, yes—but that's no excuse for *look-ing* like one!"

Their whole class was really rather proud of Dodie, because she was one of a kind; none of them had ever seen anything like her anywhere else.

Dodie was definitely the class beauty—a tall, striking blond—but at the same time she was pretty close to being the class clown, too, without ever meaning to be. Though she hadn't a shred of a sense of humor herself, she constantly said things that made everyone else laugh while she looked on in amazement, wondering what everyone thought was so funny, yet never taking offense at their laughter.

Not that Dodie was really dumb. She might have been a good student if she had tried; instead, she made the minimum effort necessary to get by. She was lazy about everything except the four great essentials: her hair, her fingernails, her eye makeup, and her clothes. In those areas no amount of effort was too much.

The business of grooming herself and thinking about clothes took up hours of her attention every day. Her saving grace was that with it all went an astonishing lack of vanity. Anyone would have thought she was a plain girl trying to make the best of what she had to work with for all the indication she ever gave to the contrary as she drifted along in her gentle, languorous way, and there was not a mean bone in her body.

When their squad of twenty-five girls assembled on a playing field in front of Miss Tingley that first day, then, Dodie was wearing a short kilt-type skirt and black knee socks and sneakers along with the rest of the group. Miss Tingley inspected them with sharp-eyed approval. She herself was a sight to behold in a long pleated skirt of uncertain vintage, as well as her own long black socks and sneakers. Her hands were folded on top of a hockey stick planted in front of her the way King Arthur might have planted his sword, Excalibur.

"Girls, I cannot tell you what satisfaction it gives me to think that at last Wagstaff High School is going to have its own field hockey team. This is long overdue. Girls' sports have been grievously neglected—but now we're going to change all that!" she predicted triumphantly, and chose to ignore a few subdued groans.

"Now, as you know, our squad is the largest of those assigned to the three fall sports. A field hockey team of eleven players is much larger than the teams needed for volley ball or—if Mr. Gluck gets his way—water polo. Therefore, a great responsibility rests on our shoulders. We must prove it worthwhile for so many of you to be devoted to our sport."

None of her listeners managed to look particularly devoted except Fran Sealey, but Miss Tingley did not let that bother her. She plunged on.

"First of all, let us get rid of certain misconceptions some of you may have as to the nature of the game. Don't confuse it with the game of ice hockey you see those savages playing on television—not that I don't occasionally enjoy that, too, in its way," she said, causing mouths to fall open. Miss Tingley watching the Bruins battle the Canadiens? Beyond belief!

"Ice hockey is an exciting game, but in many ways a crude one. Soccer is another excellent game, and all three games have the same basic structure—yet in my opinion it is field hockey which calls for the greatest finesse. In field hockey we have none of that clumsy slamming together that characterizes the other games. Understand this at once: field hockey is *not* a contact sport."

Here, at least, was some good news. Visions of cuts and bruises became less lurid in the minds of many of her listeners.

"In field hockey, bumping into an opposing player is a foul. In fact, even getting in the way of an opposing player, without so much as touching that player, can be a foul. But even more important in the area of finesse is *this*," said Miss Tingley, brandishing the hockey stick.

"Handle . . . blade . . . toe," she said, touching the three sections of the stick in turn, "and the significant thing one immediately notices about the curved part of the stick—the blade, with which we strike the ball—is that one side of the blade is flat and the other side is rounded.

"Now, in ice hockey the puck may be struck with either side of the blade. In field hockey *only* the flat side may be used—and if you don't think *that* makes for difficulties you have never played the game. The player's stick side, the side on which she strikes the ball most frequently, is her right side. Consequently all field hockey sticks are right-handed."

From the way Miss Tingley paused, it was plain she was anticipating the question several girls immediately raised in voices hopeful of reprieve.

"But, Miss Tingley, what if you're left-handed?"

"There are no left-handers in field hockey," she replied with the grim satisfaction of a teacher who had been contending with left-handers in classrooms for three generations. "You will play right-handed, and you will find it ridiculously easy to do so—indeed, your left-handedness will even become an advantage, just as it can be in golf. Left-handers should learn to play golf right-handed, because extra strength in the left arm can be a great asset there, and the same holds true for field hockey—not to mention the great help it gives in mastering the left-hand lunge. Be sure to remind me of your left-handedness, you girls who are, so that I can assign you to positions where the left-hand lunge is especially valuable."

Having crushed the southpaws' hopes, Miss Tingley clapped her hands with brisk decision.

"But now, we have stood around long enough, it's time for action. I am going to post myself on the sideline, and when I give the word I want you all to jog to the midfield line, keeping together. When you cross the midfield line I shall call out again. At that instant I want you to turn and sprint back to the goal line as hard as you can run."

Most of the girls exchanged the woebegone looks normal human beings get on their faces when suggestions of group exertion are advanced. Only Fran Sealey set herself to run in a loathsomely eager way.

"Ready! Set! Go!"

In a long ragged line the hockey squad began their fifty-yard trot up the field.

"I said jog, not plod! Pick it up! Stay with Fran! That's better!"

"Come on, come on!" Fran snapped importantly over her shoulder, already assuming the role of leader. Irma glared at her ramrod back. Almost inevitably Fran would be given such a role on sheer ability, but she might have waited.

"Turn and sprint!"

If the line had been ragged before, it was in tatters now. Fran was off like the wind. She shot into the lead with a few of the pack not far behind. Irma found herself at the finish in the second wave with most of the others.

"Terrible! Terrible! Irma, what are you doing back there? You should be able to keep up with Fran," cried Miss Tingley, and Irma glanced at Fran in time to see the superior little smirk this comment brought to the thin lips. "Now, we'll do it again, and this time when you sprint I want to see some *speed!*"

"Again?" cried Dodie in stunned disbelief, and as usual there was something about the way she said it that made everybody laugh—everybody except Miss Tingley, whose lips merely twitched.

"Again," she said, with ironic emphasis. "The game of hockey is run, run, run. At first we shall probably play short halves, only fifteen minutes each, but during that fifteen minutes nobody will be standing around. You must learn to run, and keep running. . . ."

While Miss Tingley was talking, Irma was burning. Fran needed to have that smug look wiped off her face, and Irma was going to be the eraser. This time she was going to run as hard as she could.

"Now, then—ready! Set! Go!"

Once more they jogged up the field, with considerable puffing to be heard. Irma did not so much as glance in Fran's direction, not wanting to risk putting her on her guard, but Irma's jaw was set grimly.

"Turn!"

She whirled and took off, with her first stride matching Fran's. To stimulate herself she thought about Doctor Ben's black snakes, and that helped. Ahead of everyone else, she and Fran crossed the goal line in a photo finish.

"Good work, Irma!" said Miss Tingley, and now it was Irma who could feel her face going smug while Fran gave her a hard look as though marking her for a rival.

"Dodie!"

Miss Tingley's voice cracked out, and dawdling Dodie bringing up the rear leaped forward as though a bee had just caught up with her. Puffing and blowing, the girls stood along the goal line holding their sides.

"Well, that was better. When we really get started, we won't begin with running, however. . . ."

"Good!" croaked Dodie.

"Instead, *before* we run we shall do a few limbering-up exercises—which we shall not refer to as calisthenics," Miss Tingley added with a twinkle in her ferocious old eyes, "because of course we *all* consider that a disagreeable word!"

5

While allowing her squad to take a breather, Miss Tingley issued hockey sticks, making sure each girl ended up with one the proper length and weight for her. This done, she held up a ball about the size of a baseball.

"Now this is the type of field hockey ball we shall use. It is made of a composition material, and it is hard. When you feel it you will know one reason why you wear shin guards."

She placed the ball on the ground.

"There are three basic strokes you must master—the dribble, drive, and push. Then there are the special strokes—the flick, scoop, and reverse stick. And finally there are tackles purely for defensive play—the lunge, cut, and job, or jab, as it seems to be called today. At least, such were the strokes in my time, though I am told the cut is not used much now.

"The dribble is used when you have the ball and are trying to advance it while keeping control of it," continued Miss Tingley, and surprised them by demonstrating. All at once she was running across in front of them with amazingly quick firm steps while keeping the ball just ahead of her with a series of light taps. The hand, after ever so many years, had never lost its skill.

Earlier in her talk Miss Tingley had used the same line on the class she had used on Irma, about playing back in the Devonian Period, or maybe the Cambrian. Dodie now managed to muddle it all together.

"Gee, Miss Tingley, you must have been pretty good when you were on that Devonian team!"

"You should have seen us play the Cambrian bunch," replied Miss Tingley. "We beat them four to three!"

It was things like that, of course, right in the middle of being severe and driving you to run your legs off, that made them stick with Miss Tingley.

They dribbled, drove, and pushed; they flicked, scooped, and reversed; they lunged and jabbed, and gradually their strokes became disciplined.

"But there's so much to remember!" complained Dodie later on. "Honestly, I'd almost rather study!"

They all remembered with delight Miss Tingley's comment on Dodie's handling of a hockey stick.

"Dodie, that's not an eyebrow pencil. Take a good firm grip on it!"

Dodie was quite right, however, there was an awful lot to learn. Since a player could only use one side of the blade to hit the ball with, simply getting into position to whack the thing sometimes took a whole set of gymnastic twists and turns. The limitations did indeed make play difficult. For example, if you wanted to pull the ball back to you, you had to turn your stick so that the blade faced down, then pull the ball toward you with the toe of the blade.

Worse yet, if an opponent had the ball, you could not simply charge in and knock her stick out of the way. You could only hit the ball. If you hit an opponent's stick before you had touched the ball, that was a foul.

As Dodie put it, there were more possible fouls than you could shake a stick at.

The names for things were all crazy. For example, there was the bully. The game started with a bully. This meant that the opposing center forwards squared off at midfield with the ball between them, alternately tapped the ground alongside the ball and their opponent's stick above the ball three times, then tried to hit the ball to a teammate. It was the same idea as the jump ball in basketball, only done with hockey sticks.

All these were things Irma tried to tell Marilee on the bus going home, when Marilee wasn't trying to describe Mr. Gluck's underwater torture chamber.

"I'm beat!" groaned Irma. "Absolutely beat!"

"That's nothing!" moaned Marilee. "I'm soggy!"

"I was sweaty!"

"Yes, but not waterlogged! I wish I'd never learned to swim!"

"Are you really going to play water polo?"

"If the Monster of the Deep has his way, we will!"

Mr. Gluck had collected a new nickname.

After that first day the hockey squad never ran again without hockey sticks in their hands.

"You must learn how to carry your stick and not let it get in your way while running at full tilt," said Miss Tingley. "You may carry it across your body in both hands, or at your side with one hand holding it in the middle, just so long as you can instantly bring it into position if you have a chance to field and hit the ball. And you must learn never to let any part of your stick rise higher than the level of your shoulders. That is called 'sticks,' or 'making sticks,' and is a foul. Both sticks and the ball should stay close to the ground. Anything else can be dangerous."

Field and hit the ball—that was a typical example of the finesse of the game Miss Tingley talked so much about. When the ball came your way you didn't just take a swipe at it, which would probably send it in the wrong direction, anyway; instead you "fielded" it—stopped it and got it under control—and *then* decided what to do with it, either dribble it or pass it to a teammate.

"Of course, if you try to dribble the ball, the opponent who is marking you will tackle," said Miss Tingley, using two puzzling terms, both of them alarming. It turned out, however, that to "mark" an opposing player did not mean to inflict a scar. It meant staying close to that player so as to intercept passes if possible or tackle if the player got the ball. And "tackle" meant trying to take the ball away from the opposing player.

Tackling was where the lunge and jab came in, and again the difficulty was that you could only use the flat side of your blade, no matter what angle you were trying to reach the ball from.

If an opponent controlled the ball, you couldn't step in front of her with your shoulder in her way—that was obstruction, another foul.

Because of this there was even something called the circular tackle, which involved circling in front of your opponent in order to get into position to take the ball away from her. This could be like trying to run around in a circle in front of an express train, but since someone trying to control the ball could seldom run as fast as someone who was simply running, it could be done.

For a game that involved nothing more than some curved sticks and a ball, there was an awful lot to learn.

By then, too, they heard that Hyde Park High had also fielded a hockey squad, and that on top of everything else, one of these days they would have to play them in an interschool game!

At their third practice session Miss Tingley turned up with a young woman whom she introduced as Mrs. Dora Draper.

"Mrs. Draper has kindly volunteered to assist me, for which I am most grateful," announced Miss Tingley. "She too has played hockey—a good deal more recently than I have, I hardly need add. Her help will make all our tasks a great deal easier."

Mrs. Draper was a pretty young woman with large, dewy eyes and a sweet, ineffectual expression. She proved to be an ideal assistant, always ready to follow Miss Tingley's lead. Her easygoing manner nicely complemented Miss Tingley's drive. Even though she was not very forceful about anything, it was plain she did know a lot about hockey.

Being well aware that practice alone, however necessary, was not enough to hold interest, Miss Tingley announced that on Monday they would divide into teams and hold their first scrimmage. The news was all Fran Sealey needed to start looking ahead.

"We haven't any time to lose," she declared as a group of them were walking back to their locker room from the field. "We've got to start getting up for our big game!"

"What do you mean, our big game? Our *only* game!" scoffed Irma, and got herself a dirty look.

"It's still our big game!"

"We haven't got a chance," sighed someone. "Hyde Park is twice as big a school as we are."

"That doesn't mean they have to be twice as good!" Fran insisted in her poisonously gung-ho way.

"Well, anyway, we've got a secret weapon," said Angie Minelli.

"What?"

"Miss Tingley!"

There was something in that, of course.

6 _____

"How many of you girls have a red sweater or blouse?" Miss Tingley had asked at the end of the last practice session.

More than half the squad raised their hands, but not Irma, and not Dodie.

"Dodie Fenwick, why isn't your hand up? If you don't own a red sweater or blouse, as well as one of every other color in the rainbow, I don't have two eyes!"

"Well, gee, Miss Tingley," said Dodie fearfully, "I was afraid it was some kind of trick!"

"Then you can relax. I am merely trying to put two teams on the field who can tell each other apart," said Miss Tingley, and quickly chose twelve girls, including Dodie, who were to bring their red sweaters or blouses.

Irma found herself at right inner on the Blue team, as Miss Tingley called it "simply for purposes of identification," and she was glad to be there, because Fran Sealey was on the Red team. And Fran was the Red team's center forward, which meant she was the one who kept an eye on the forward line and warned her teammates when they were out of position or off side—in other words, Fran would have almost limitless opportunities to be bossy.

Irma was delighted to be on the Blue team, where instead of taking orders from Fran she would have a chance to botch up Fran's game plan in every way she could. At right inner she would not be directly opposed to Fran (the center half marked the opposing center forward defensively), but she intended to give her all the trouble she could.

The forward line—the offensive players—consisted of left wing, left inner, center forward, right inner, and right wing. The other six players were defensive: left half, center half, right half, left and right fullbacks, and goalkeeper.

Their head coach's selection of goalies had been a surprise. Everybody expected her to choose the two biggest and brawniest girls on the squad, but instead she chose Bunky Bergman and Martha Grimes, both of whom were small but lively as crickets.

"It isn't size a goalie needs, it's agility. Agility, courage, and determination, and I know I can count on Bunky and Martha for all those qualities. The goalie is all-important. Without a good goalie no team can hope to win," explained Miss Tingley, causing both girls to feel instant pride in their selection where a moment before they had been long-faced. And then she added a postscript that made them objects of envy. "Oh, yes—and the goalies should wear jeans instead of kilts, to prevent chafing by the straps of their leg pads."

Mrs. Draper stationed herself on the field, ready to run back and forth as the umpire. Miss Tingley paced the sidelines, whistle in hand.

"Very well, let's begin. Line up for the center bully, girls!"

Mrs. Draper placed the ball on the center of the fifty-yard line at midfield. The teams took their positions, forwards spaced out on each side of the line, backs dotted down the field in a slightly oblique pattern, goalies in front of their cages. The center forwards, Fran Sealey and Angie Minelli, squared off on each side of the ball. Three times they tapped the ground alongside the ball and each other's sticks above the ball, and the scrimmage was underway.

Angie tried hard, but Fran was quicker. She

got possession of the ball and cleared it with a short pass to her left inner, Linda Katz. Since the left side of one team faced the right side of the other, Irma was opposite Linda. Irma rushed forward to try a straight, oncoming tackle, and Linda tried to pass—but then play became indescribable, because at least six other players converged on the ball. Sticks clattered on sticks and—if sharp yelps were any indication—tested two or three shin guards, one of them being Irma's.

Wheeeeeeee!

Miss Tingley's whistle blasted the melee to a halt. She came trotting out with her eyes flashing fire in all directions.

"Girls, girls! This is a hockey match, not a barroom brawl! I saw at least twelve fouls before I lost count—but worse still, what did you think you were doing, all pitching in that way? When even three are after the ball at the same time there's something wrong! Play your position! Keep your distance. Give your teammate a chance to pass. Be ready to intercept a pass if the opponent tackles successfully and gets the ball—and being ready means marking the opposing player you're *supposed* to mark! Sally and Maureen, you're both backs—what were *you* doing up here?"

There was a lot more of this—it was astonishing how much Miss Tingley had observed in the space of a few seconds—and then she called on her assistant.

"Have you anything to add before we try again, Mrs. Draper?"

Mrs. Draper passed around one of her soothing smiles.

"No, I don't think so. I'm sure the girls will do better next time."

Again they lined up for the center bully, and this time they found new ways of doing everything wrong. Both center forwards managed to hit the ball, but it bounced off Angie's blade in the direction of the Red center half, who fielded it and drove a long pass toward her right wing, Hazel Hoff. Hazel got her stick ready and watched the ball come to her, while the rest of them sort of stood around waiting to see what would happen.

Wheeeeeeee!

"When I say play your positions, that doesn't mean you're to stay rooted to the spot! When a pass comes your way, Hazel, run toward it, get to the ball as fast as you can. As for you, Nan," she said, singling out Blue's left half, "rush forward and try to intercept. *Everyone* should be in motion, the Blues trying to cover, the Reds trying to make spaces so that Hazel will have someone to pass to. Let's try again, and this time we'll keep play going no matter *how* bad it is!"

The third time things went a little better. The

ball began to move up and down the field. And Fran began to be heard from, ordering the Red forwards about, and even getting after the center half.

"Mary! Mark Angie!" The center half was supposed to mark the opposing center forward. And when Mary not only marked, but tackled and got the ball, another order cracked out— "Clear it to wing!" It did not take Fran long to pick up the terms, of course.

Mary managed to push a square pass in the direction of the sideline, where Dodie was supposedly playing left half, and Dodie did actually run a few steps in the direction of the ball. She looked very much as if she intended to field it and hit it, but as she drew her stick back she suddenly froze. She held up one hand, fingers stretched wide, and stared at it in horror, while the ball rolled past and over the sideline.

Wheeeeeeee!

"Dodie, what's the matter? Are you hurt?"

By now Dodie was looking vastly relieved.

"No, I'm all right!"

"Then for heaven's sake, girl, don't stop in the middle of a stroke!"

"But, Miss Tingley!" cried Dodie, "I thought I had broken a fingernail!"

After that, under the lash of their head coach's capable tongue, even Dodie got moving. The scrimmage proceeded, and bit by bit some of the tactics they were supposed to use began to make sense. It even became sort of exciting the first time the Blue team managed to get down close to the striking circle.

Marked off in front of each cage was a sixteen-yard semicircle. This was the striking circle. Only shots for goal hit on or inside that circle counted. If someone hit the ball past the opponent's goalie and into the cage, it did not count as a goal if the ball had been shot from outside the circle.

The ball came down the field to Blue's left wing, who pushed a short pass to her left inner, who reached back for it and got off a lucky pass to Angie just inside the striking circle. Angie had her first chance at a goal.

Out on the Red twenty-five-yard line Fran was in agony, judging from her tone of voice.

"Stop them, Bunky!" she screamed at the Red goalie, and it was plainly all Fran could do not to rush into the circle and try to stop them herself. But the defense of the goal was up to the defensive players. The forward line's job was to stay out near the twenty-five-yard line, ready to receive a pass if the defenders managed to get control of the ball and clear it out of the circle. They could not have helped, anyway, because too many defenders jammed inside the circle, stumbling over each other, were as bad as too few.

The most important defender was the goalie, and it was essential not to obstruct the goalie's line of sight of the ball. The goalie had the best chance of preventing a goal, because she could use her legs, feet, stick, or hand to stop the ball.

Her legs were protected by canvas pads that tripled the breadth of her legs. When the goalie crouched slightly, holding these pads together, they presented a solid wall that was very effective in blocking shots. It was not enough simply to stop the ball, however; she still had to clear it, and for that purpose she had only two weapons, her feet or her stick.

She could stop the ball with her hand but not throw it or push it away; but she was permitted to kick it away, and wore canvas kickers over her sneakers to protect her feet when she stopped the ball or kicked it. Her feet were her best defensive weapon, even though there were times when she could clear the ball quickest with her stick.

Angie hit a hard shot for goal, and Irma rushed in along with Blue's left inner, because the inners were supposed to rush every shot for goal in hopes of hitting the ball again and quickly scoring should the first attempt be stopped by a defender. But Bunky Bergman had practiced hard at her blocking and clearing and now her efforts paid off. She stopped the ball with her left foot and kicked it to the left with her right foot so quickly it went past Irma out of reach and straight to Dodie, the Red left half, who happened to be loitering around nearby.

Dodie looked down at the ball in horror. It was easy to read her mind. "Gracious! The sooner I hit it, the sooner it will be gone!" She swung at it wildly and hit it exactly where she should never, never have hit it—straight across the field in front of her own goal mouth. A defender should never clear the ball that way, because that puts the ball squarely in front of the goal where the other team can get another crack at shooting for a score.

Everybody was so dumfounded to see Dodie hit the ball at all, however, that it shot across the field past the whole Blue attack and Red defense in the striking circle and was fielded by the Red right half, who passed to her own right wing and sent the Red line charging down the field with a chance of their own.

The ball finally came to Fran inside the Blue circle at a tough angle and she made a desperate try for goal but just missed. The ball went over the goal line outside the cage and was brought out to the sixteen-yard-line for a defense hit to start play again.

Watching Fran as she turned back with a ridiculously grim, disappointed expression after missing goal, Irma suddenly understood what Fran's trouble was.

She wanted to be first to score a goal!

Perversely, Irma's own expression changed.

"Well, we'll see about that!" she muttered, and settled down to play for blood.

It took some time before she had a chance to do anything. But finally Blue's right wing picked up a pass well downfield, dribbled along the sideline, and drove the ball in to Irma near the striking circle.

Angie was charging in close by and was clear. Irma got off a sharp push to her and Angie pulled a fast one. As quick as a cat she turned squarely toward Irma as Irma moved, and hit the ball straight back to her. Irma's pass had drawn the goalie Angie's way, leaving the side of the cage open. The rest was as easy as putting a crab apple between two trees.

There was considerable Blue cheering, of course, as her teammates gathered around Irma in a suitable imitation of hockey players on television. Over someone's shoulder she caught a glimpse of Fran out on the twenty-five-yard line turning away with an absolutely bitter expression.

At that point play stopped for a spell while Miss Tingley lectured them about all the things they had done wrong. Mrs. Draper even added a few points that showed how much she really knew about the game.

The extra girls on the squad were sent into the scrimmage in place of three of the girls who seemed most winded—needless to say, these did not include Dodie Fenwick. Play resumed, and Miss Tingley soon had them hopping. All sorts of commands filled the air.

"Move, Dodie, move! Defense, clear the ball to the sides! Offense, use a straight-through pass! Dodie, cover! Come on, Red team, use your wings!"

"I wish I had some!" panted poor Dodie in Irma's ear.

"Dodie! What are you doing here?"

"Oh, dear! Am I in the wrong place again? See you later!" said Dodie, and rushed off in the wrong direction.

Red got into scoring position after a while and the Blue goalie, Martha Grimes, committed a foul by batting the ball away with her hand, which called for a penalty stroke. While Martha stood ready on the goal line in front of the cage, an opposing player tried a shot for goal, using either a push, flick, or scoop, from a point seven yards in front of the cage. Fran made the try and managed to flick the ball past Martha into the net, at which point practice ended for the day. Fran had finally scored—but at least she had not scored first, and had not scored in regular play, Irma reflected with mean pleasure.

I'm a stinker, she thought to herself, and I'm enjoying it!

The next time they turned out for practice every girl on the Blue team was wearing a blue sweater or blouse.

7

Miss Tingley knew how to put the carrot in front of the donkey. Most of the girls had really enjoyed the scrimmage. They looked forward to more of the same. So now, before she allowed them to play, she drove them through practice drills harder than ever. They practiced dribbling. They practiced exchanging passes. They practiced dodging and tackling. And practice, as someone put it, was drab. The word went the rounds—drab! drab! drab!—and finally reached their coach's sharp ears.

"Of course practice is drab," she snapped, and

pointed to Linda Katz. "Linda, you've been taking piano lessons for years. How would you describe the routine of practicing your scales?"

"Drab!"

"Of course. But without first practicing your scales you could never have mastered that splendid Rachmaninoff prelude you played for us at our last assembly. Anything worth doing is worth doing well, and anything worth doing well involves hard work!"

So they practiced. But then, just when they were getting thoroughly sick of it, they would be allowed a good scrimmage. Each time their play improved. Everyone tried hard, and the better they played the more fun the scrimmages were. They even began to think of themselves as either Reds or Blues.

Miss Tingley let this go on for one or two more practice sessions and then lowered the boom.

"Gather round, girls," she ordered after a spirited scrimmage during which the Blues had outscored the Reds and at the end of which there had been a lot of "Yea, Blues!" cheering going on. She looked at them sternly, and named off several of the Blue players, including Irma and Angie. "I want you girls to show up next time wearing a bit of red—anything will do. Red, but nothing blue."

She named several of the Red players and told them to wear something blue next time instead of their red sweaters. She switched about half of each side to the other and, disregarding their groans, explained the move.

"We're not here to create two teams, we're here to create *one* team," she told them. "That must be our aim from this point on, because our game with Hyde Park has now been set. Games, I should say, since we will meet twice, once on our field and once on theirs. We will be David against Goliath, but we must make a good showing. After all, David did," she added with a spirited twinkle in her eye.

"When is our first game?" asked Fran eagerly.

Miss Tingley named the date, and they gasped.

"Yes, indeed. Since today is Friday, we have just two weeks in which to be ready. Starting with our next session, we shall have to go all out!"

"Gee, I thought we already had been!" said Dodie.

Miss Tingley chuckled.

"Then we shall have to go all outer!"

As they straggled away to the locker room there was some griping about the changes, of course.

"It isn't fair! She gave Red our best forwards and let them keep their best ones!" grumbled Winky Davis, a loyal Blue who had not been switched.

"Yes, but you got Mary Margolis, who's a terrific center half, and Daisy Chang at right half-back, and you got to keep you and Nan Pratt—and you got Bunky, who's the best goalie," a Red retorted.

"Yes, and you didn't get *me*," Dodie pointed out in her serious way.

Then Irma had a flash of perception.

"Hey, you know what she's done? She's put the best forward line on one team and the best backfield on the other."

"I was just going to say that," declared Fran Sealey in an authoritative tone of voice. "What's more, she'll keep shifting us around now until by the time of our game with Hyde Park, we'll have a first team lined up."

"And I'll be on the bench," said Dodie happily.

Irma glanced at Fran's thin, arrogant face and gritted her teeth. From now on she would have to listen to her instead of Angie and Fran would love it, every minute of it. Even though Angie had been switched to the Red team, Irma was sure Miss Tingley would keep Fran at center forward and put Angie somewhere else on the line. In all fairness, she would be crazy if she didn't.

Whether anyone liked it or not, Fran was the best.

Their next scrimmage started off as a rather slow affair, with half of each team feeling out of place and almost like traitors, but before long the situation became interesting and play picked up.

Offensively the action was one-sided, with the Red line controlling the ball most of the time; yet almost every time they battled their way into the striking circle, Blue's defense was too much for them. On the other hand, although Blue's line was weak, Red's defense was weaker. Scoring remained about even. Irma had been right about Miss Tingley's strategy.

Their scrimmage time was nearly over for the day when a push-in by Daisy Chang didn't suit their head coach and she stopped play to explain what was wrong. When the ball went out of bounds, the team that had not hit it out pushed or flicked it in again from the point where it had gone out. Many of the push-ins were taken by the wing backs—in this case, the right halfback.

"No, no, Daisy, *everybody* could tell which way you were going to send the ball that time," called Miss Tingley as she hurried down the sideline. In her eagerness to reach the place where play had stopped and make her point, she failed to notice a hockey stick someone had left in the grass near the sideline. She stepped on it, twisted sideways, and fell.

A dozen other hockey sticks dropped from Red and Blue hands, and in seconds she was surrounded by girls reaching down to help her up. But Miss Tingley raised one hand in a gesture that stopped them. Her face was white with pain, but she was her usual composed self.

"No, don't touch me, girls."

She turned to Mrs. Draper, who had dropped to one knee beside her.

"Dora, will you run in and see if you can find the nurse and ask her if she can come out for a moment? Perhaps she had better bring a stretcher—yes, I'm afraid she'd better ask a couple of the men to help."

Miss Tingley shook her head, deeply annoyed with herself.

"What a clumsy fool I am! I'm very much afraid I have broken something."

She was right. She had broken her leg. And such was her prominence that the Saturday morning edition of the local newspaper carried quite an item about the accident written by the editor himself, who had once sat in her classroom and who still prided himself on having sweated out a B in his senior year.

During the next week men and women all over the country, some of whom were gray-haired themselves now, opened letters with the clipping enclosed, read it and remembered their old teacher and made appropriate comments.

"Good grief! At her age, coaching a hockey team! Sounds just like her!"

According to her doctor, she would not be able

to return to her classes for several weeks—and furthermore, would "not be allowed to, not if I have to strap her down!" the editor, doubtless with great glee, quoted her doctor as saying. Irma was surprised when she read the doctor's name.

"So she's another patient Doctor Ben hasn't given up," she remarked.

"Probably couldn't if he wanted to," said her father. "He's probably been her doctor for forty years, and people like Miss Tingley don't care to change doctors."

Later on that morning, when Irma was riding around the village on her bike, she saw Doctor Ben's car coming down Sea Street. She hailed him. He stopped and beamed out at her.

"Hi, Irma. How's the knee?"

"Terrible. How are the snakes?"

"Well, they've mostly retired for the winter—but they always ask for you. But what was it you wanted, Irma?"

"Are you really Miss Tingley's doctor?"

He nodded. "Have been for more years than I care to remember."

"Well, is she going to be all right?"

"That depends on what you mean by all right. As a patient she'll be her usual cantankerous self. But her leg will heal properly. You know her. It wouldn't dare do otherwise."

"But she won't be back for several weeks?"

"Not if I can help it. The only thing I can predict with confidence is that she'll be back sooner than I want her to be. If she had her way she'd hop in a wheelchair and be back in her classroom on Monday—but she's not going to be."

"And I guess she'll be out of hockey for the rest of the season."

"That much I *can* guarantee you. 'Hermione,' I told her, 'I categorically forbid you to go near that field again until *I* give the okay,' and I meant it. How's the hockey going, by the way?"

"Well, it *was* going okay," Irma admitted. "I mean, with her pushing everybody around and making everybody jump and things like that, it was sort of fun, but. . . ."

"Well, I'm sure things will work out all right. From what I hear of your Ms. Cranshaw she won't let your athletic program sag just because one of her warriors has fallen by the wayside. Take care of that knee!"

Irma watched him drive off, then swung her bike around and headed slowly for home. In front of her, as she turned into South Street, a few last survivors of the crab-apple crop still dotted the sides of the road. On an impulse she braked to a stop, leaned her bike against a tree, and took Old Faithful from its place. Might as well finish off the season.

She could not help thinking how differently she handled the stick now, hitting only from one side. Dribbling an apple up the blacktop and flicking it expertly between the two trees, she recalled that day Miss Tingley had pounced on her right here. Soon she was laughing rather sadly at the memory. She felt a vague depression that went beyond mere concern for Miss Tingley, and did not understand what was worrying her until much later.

8 _____

When the girls assembled for their first practice session after the accident, Mrs. Draper made a little speech. With her head on one side and an uncertain appeal in her gentle eyes, she twittered away at some length.

"I'm sure we all feel equally sad about losing our head coach," she said, making it sound as if Miss Tingley had passed into the Great Beyond, "but I'm sure we will carry on as if she were here. We don't want to let her down, do we? So let's practice hard, and show her we can do it. I'll need the help and cooperation of every one of you, and I'm sure I can count on it. So . . .

shall we get started? Why don't we begin today with a triangular pass drill?"

They trotted out obediently to form lines, but Linda Katz muttered, "That was some pep talk. More like a memorial service."

There was not much spark in any of their efforts that day, and Mrs. Draper showed little ability to do much about correcting things on her own. Mostly she ran around with hands dangling from wrists and with an apologetic look on her pretty face as she uttered cries that were more like wails of despair than sharp comments.

From that day forward their practice sessions went steadily downhill. Girls began to clown around and goof off. Their lazy scrimmages were good for laughs but not much else. Poor Mrs. Draper scuttled about squawking and scolding in wishy-washy ways that had little effect on anyone. Someone hung the nickname of Droopy Draper on her, and of course it caught on at once.

Irma and Angie and a few others still made some effort to play well, but it was hard to keep at it when the majority of the girls were loafing. Only Fran continued to drive herself hard every moment and snap at the loafers and make herself generally unpopular—more unpopular, that is to say.

"How are we going to look against Hyde Park, if we play like this?" she cried angrily after a scrimmage that had been a comedy of errors.

"Oh, who cares about Hyde Park?" sniffed one of the worst offenders. "I'll bet they're not working at it any harder than we are. The whole thing is a farce, anyway."

"Maybe it will rain," said Dodie.

The heavens did not oblige, however. The day of the game arrived under clear skies. The Hyde Park team turned up on schedule, with every girl wearing not only a kilt but also green bib-like affairs Mrs. Draper referred to as "pinnies," which seemed to be short for pinafore. The Wagstaff girls were all wearing some touch of red.

During their last few practices Mrs. Draper had put together a first team that was pretty much what they had expected—Red's forward line and Blue's backfield. This combination had made mincemeat of the weaker second team in their easygoing scrimmages, causing some of the optimists among them to predict they would give Hyde Park a surprise.

The Wagstaff squad had never gotten as far as thinking about a captain, but Hyde Park had one, a tall girl with long auburn hair who played center half. Her name was Lally Beecham. She was almost as pretty as Dodie, and her arrogance made Fran Sealey look meek.

When they met at midfield to start the game, she was poisonously patronizing.

"We're glad to have a chance to practice against another team," she said with a sweet smile. "We're tired of beating our three scrub teams."

Three scrub teams! That meant they had at least twice as many girls out for hockey as Wagstaff. The girls they had brought along represented only about half of their total squad.

The game had not been underway for two minutes before it was plain Hyde Park had received some competent coaching. The woman with the iron-gray hair who was pacing the sideline in front of their bench did not seem to provide the sort of inspirational fire Miss Tingley could produce, but she knew what she was doing, and she was firm and crisp about it.

Before three minutes were up, one of Hyde Park's inners had slipped past Wagstaff's confused defense and hammered home a goal. A couple of minutes later only a great save by Bunky prevented a second goal, and after that the roof fell in.

By half time the score was already 5 to 0, and Fran was almost in tears—except of course that Fran would not allow herself to cry. As for poor Droopy, when she tried to summon up material for the standard half-time pep talk, she looked pretty miserable herself. She looked like a woman who wished she had never played hockey, or at least had never been so foolish as to volunteer her help at Wagstaff.

"Of course they have many advantages, with

their huge squad and all, and they haven't had anything happen to their head coach—Mrs. Carmichael is her name, and I understand she once coached hockey at a girls' college," said Droopy Draper, piling up all the negative points with a masterful hand, all the points that would help them find excuses for themselves. Irma thought almost longingly of Miss Tingley at that moment. The things *she* would have had to say about their performance! Not one of them would have had an inch of skin left on her back—but they would have returned to the field in a different frame of mind from the one Droopy was creating with her milk-toast approach.

Even Droopy recognized that a little fighting talk was in order, that she could not finish without at least making the attempt. So she firmed up her rather unprominent chin as much as she could and got down to it.

"However, let's remember what Miss Tingley said about David and Goliath. Let's go out there this time and do the very best we can and make her proud of us!"

This was not much, but it was something. Not, however, enough. It was still a demoralized team that took the field for the second half—and a team that was paying the price for its sins.

Because the girls had been loafing during so many recent practice sessions, they were not in the proper condition. First-string players had tired to the point of becoming useless and had to be replaced by the second-stringers. Wagstaff did not quite get down to Dodie, but came close. The team tried harder than it had in the first half, but it was too late. Hyde Park rolled over them.

The final score was 11 to 0. Once or twice Fran had nearly reached the striking circle, but both times Lally Beecham, whose job it was to mark the opposing center forward, had managed to tackle well enough to get the ball out of her control. Once Irma actually had a shot inside the circle but just missed the far side of the cage. And the goalie successfully kicked away Angie's sole try for goal.

When the horn hooted the end of the game, Irma was near Fran and Lally Beecham. Lally's laugh tinkled in their ears, and she waved her hand airily.

"Thanks for the practice!" she said, and ran off with a smirk on her face that made Fran and Irma turn and glance at each other, except that this time they were not really glaring at each other, but sharing a glare. Neither of them said a word as they trudged off toward the sideline, but each knew what the other was thinking.

As the team came in from the field to join the rest of the squad in front of the benches on the Wagstaff side, nobody was having much to say. Mrs. Draper was automatically superintending the gathering-up of extra equipment, making sure nothing was left behind. Then Nan Pratt remembered something, and was obviously glad she had.

"Oh, Mrs. Draper, I won't be able to come to practice Monday. I have to go to my grandmother's for her birthday and we're leaving early."

"All right, Nan. I'm not sure about Monday, anyway. I mean—well. . . ."

Everyone grew suddenly silent as Mrs. Draper turned and swept her eyes around the group. She looked pretty dismal, but at least for once she didn't look wishy-washy.

"I'm not sure what the arrangements will be on Monday. I—I don't know what you girls need, but you need something more than I can give you. So . . . at any rate, just check the bulletin board Monday morning. There will be an announcement. All right, shall we go?"

She turned away rather quickly and led the group toward the school buildings, a group of girls silently exchanging wide-eyed glances.

"Well, it suits me fine if Droopy quits and we don't have any more hockey," Irma told Marilee the next morning. "It's a bore anyway."

"You really think you won't have to play anymore?"

"Well, we can't have a team without a coach."

Marilee sighed.

"Some people have all the luck! Nothing ever happens to the Monster! Was your game really that bad?"

"Awful. We were rotten. I'm just glad nobody came to watch."

"Well, at least that's one good thing about Ms. Cranshaw, she's not drumming up crowds," said Marilee, and mimicked their assistant principal. " 'Our program is not intended to draw spectators or encourage competition to any significant extent, but merely to provide you girls with a chance at healthy participation in team sports.' "

"Well, she didn't have to worry," said Irma. "Nobody came."

9

Irma always remembered that next Monday as the day of surprises.

In the first place, when she got to school that morning, there was a notice on the bulletin board which simply said:

> Field hockey practice will be
> held as usual at 3:00 P.M.
>   D. Draper

When she went to her locker Irma found several of the girls talking about the notice, but none of them, not even Fran Sealey, had any idea what it meant.

"I suppose Miss Tingley talked her into finishing the season," said Daisy. "After all, it's only three weeks till our second game with Hyde Park and then it will all be over."

Fran was disgusted.

"Well, if this means three more weeks of flubbing around in the same old way, then as far as I'm concerned—well, I wish I could transfer to another sport!"

The first surprise was nothing, however, compared to the second one. They went to their first-period English class expecting to see their substitute teacher behind the desk. Instead they saw a wheelchair beside the desk with Miss Tingley in it.

Her right leg was stretched out in a fearsome cast on a platform in front of her, and a ruthlessly triumphant smile was on her face.

The girls entered the room behind a boy named Harold Burbank, who was an excitable type. Harold nearly jumped out of his skin.

"My gosh! Miss Tingley, what are you doing here?"

"Good morning, Harold. I am doing what I usually do when I come to this room. I am meeting my classes. Take your seat, Harold, and pull yourself together."

When they were all in their places and the first bell had sounded, she explained her presence.

"I have sat around at home as long as I can stand it. It took some doing, but I finally convinced my doctor that I can sit here just as well."

Irma had to suppress a giggle. She could imagine what Doctor Ben had been through.

"After all, I don't teach English composition and literature with my leg. I don't mark papers with my toes," continued Miss Tingley. "Even my doctor had to admit that."

"But how do you get into a car?"

"Friends who own an ideally suitable pickup truck have volunteered their help. They are able to back the truck quite close to my back porch, and luckily the truck's interior floor is very nearly on the same level. A three-by-six sheet of half-inch plywood makes an excellent bridge both there and for the loading platform at the rear of the school, where again the difference between the two levels is luckily quite negligible. And inside, of course, there is the service elevator," she said, and added with a grim smile, "I had plenty of time to work out the details in my mind while sitting around idly these past weeks."

"Past weeks?" said Angie Minelli's twin brother Larry. "Gee, Miss Tingley, you've only been gone *two!*"

"Under some circumstances, Larry, two weeks can seem like two months."

"Like hockey practice," suggested Dodie in her wide-eyed earnest way.

Miss Tingley's eyes fired up dangerously.

"Yes, indeed. I have heard about how things have been going on the hockey field. I have had a full report. Something will have to be done about that. Something will definitely have to be done about that. But now, we are not here to discuss field hockey, we are here to discuss English literature. Open your books to page sixty-two."

When class was over, speculation was rife among the girls.

"I'll bet she really lit a fire under poor Droopy!"

"How do you light a fire under a wet blanket?"

"Well, something must have happened. Droopy must be going to carry on, because she signed that notice."

"Incredible!" said Dodie. "I never thought I'd see the day when I could hardly wait for hockey practice!"

The young woman who was waiting for them when the squad turned out for practice looked quite different from the dispirited figure that had drooped away to her car after the Friday disaster. A little smile, almost a grin, was tugging away at her Cupid's-bow lips. Mrs. Draper was almost perky. When they had all gathered around, she had a few words to say.

"Girls, I have agreed to continue as your assistant coach, because some splendid help has been arranged for you. I know I'm not cut out to be your head coach, but I think I can carry on if I have the right backing—and I'm going to have that now."

So saying, she waved her hand in the direction of the east wing of the school, which was not far from the field.

"All right, girls, now give me your attention!"

A familiar voice with a sinister rasp added to it assailed their ears in stentorian tones. Every girl whirled around to look. There, at an open window, with field glasses in one hand and a bullhorn in the other, sat Miss Tingley.

"Good afternoon, girls. Now, Mrs. Draper and I have had a long talk about your disgraceful performance against Hyde Park. Though she blames herself, I do not. It is plain to me that you have responded to her kind efforts by taking advantage in every way lazy, shiftless girls could think of. You have shirked your job, you have been silly and irresponsible, and last Friday you paid the price. So now we are going to change all that.

"Winning is not necessary, but playing to the very best of our abilities is. You may not beat Hyde Park the next time you play them, but you are going to make a decent showing, and I am going to be right here to see that you are prepared to do so."

She paused, and the mere ghost of a sly chuckle seemed to escape her as she went on.

"As I am sure you know, my doctor has forbidden me to come near the field. He allowed me to return to school only if I would promise not to leave the building except to go home. I cannot, however, see how he could possibly object to my sitting here with my bird-watching field glasses and this voice-amplification contraption Mr. Gluck has been kind enough to lend me. So let's get started. Get the girls lined up, Dora, and we'll begin with some—yes, this time I'll come right out with the ugly word—*calisthenics!*"

By the time she had run them through a few brisk limbering-up exercises they were panting. By the time they had practiced dribbling and dodging and passing, they were sweating. And before they had been scrimmaging for very long, their tongues were hanging out.

"Dodie! Don't wait for the ball, run to it! Move!" And Dodie moved. Joyously they labored under their head coach's lash, knowing very well they were getting what they deserved. And once again, curiously enough, hockey was fun.

When Irma, tired but happy—at least, she kept breaking into a giggle and even laughing out loud when she thought about one thing and another that had happened during that crazy practice—when Irma dragged up the road and came into the house, her mother had a message for her.

"Doctor Fulton phoned," she said worriedly.

"He wants you to call him. He sounded upset. He—"

Irma whooped.

"I'll bet I know what it is!" she cried, and rushed to the phone. Seeing Irma so merry about it all made her mother look relieved.

"I thought maybe someone was ill."

"If anyone is, it's him!"

Doctor Ben answered so promptly it was plain he had been fretting around the phone.

"Hello!"

"Hi. Mom said you wanted to talk to me."

"Well, I certainly wanted to talk to *somebody!* I've been calling *her* number for an hour but she doesn't answer. She knows darn well it's me calling! Listen, Irma, is it true what someone called up to tell me, or were they just pulling my leg?"

"Somebody's a dirty stool pigeon," said Irma.

"Then it's true! You mean to tell me that stubborn old fool planted herself at an open window—"

"She was all bundled up."

"Never mind how she was bundled up! At an open window, with her field glasses and a bullhorn, and coached your hockey practice?"

"Yes, and she was great! You should have seen the way she got things going again! She even had Dodie Fenwick hopping like mad!"

"Dodie Fenwick?" said the doctor, impressed in spite of himself. "Well, never mind that, the point is she's pulled a fast one, and I'm sure she's just tickled to death with herself. As far as I'm concerned, she can get herself another doctor!"

"Gosh, would you really tell her to do that?"

Doctor Ben responded with a gloomy sigh.

"No, I suppose not. Over the years I've already done that twelve or thirteen times. It never works."

"Well, don't worry. I'll bet she'll manage just fine. And we really need her, if we're going to make a decent showing against Hyde Park next time—that's what she says we've got to do, make a decent showing. We only have three weeks to get ready. Oh, and that's another thing. Our second game is at Hyde Park. Do you think that in another two weeks she'll be able to go with us to—"

An alarming sputter interrupted her, as if a fuse were blowing somewhere along the line.

"What? Irma Tuttle, are you off your— Go to Hyde Park for a hockey game in *two weeks?*"

She could actually hear him draw in a huge breath, after which he thundered out a grand pronouncement.

"Over . . . my . . . dead . . . body!"

10

Unorthodox though it might be, their new coaching system proved effective. The quality of the Wagstaff squad's performance rapidly improved. There was something about the very nuttiness of being bellowed at by an old lady from a window that made them giggle and grin and give their all. A lifetime of bird-watching stood Miss Tingley in good stead. She could zero those field glasses in on any player's slightest movement in a split second. Nothing seemed to escape her. Nobody was safe.

"I *never* get to slow down anymore!" complained Dodie. "I hardly have a chance to draw a breath. When I get through being pushed around by *her* all afternoon, my mascara's all runny and my hair looks like a bird's nest!"

If the new system was a shot in the arm to the players, it was a shot in both arms to Dora Draper. For one thing she was no longer as ineffectual as she had been. The terrible experience of going through the Hyde Park disaster had done something for her. That, in combination with the lifeline Miss Tingley had thrown her, seemed to have given her new backbone. Then, too, because of the way she had handled herself, the girls could not help but like her better. And since she sensed this, she became more self-confident. She even began to bark at them a little herself and take less nonsense from them. References to Droopy became fewer and fewer. The nickname seemed to fade away. Among themselves she became Drape, or even Dora, but somewhere along the line Droopy dropped by the wayside.

During that period there was a great deal of talk about athletics among Irma and Marilee and one or two other girls on their bus. According to Marilee, life in the pool was still dreadful.

"Are you going to play Hyde Park?" asked Irma.

"No. Not Hyde Park or anyone else. Nobody else is crazy enough to have a water polo team. But that doesn't bother the Monster. He says this way we have a chance of getting through the season undefeated. Funny, funny!"

A couple of days later, however, the water polo picture changed.

"Some smart-aleck sophomores are getting a team together and are going to challenge us to a game! Mr. Gluck says they'll be bigger but we'll be smarter. So we're going to have a game after all!"

Marilee turned to Laurie Murdoch in the seat behind them.

"Gee, Laurie, you're lucky you're in volleyball!"

"What do you mean, lucky?" cried Laurie. "You have no idea how difficult volleyball is to play creatively—that's what Miss Fletcher calls it, playing creatively. It's not at all like that primitive backyard stuff where people just bat the ball back and forth and make silly remarks. There's strategy and tactics and—and teamwork, and—well, all sorts of things!"

They were not able to get in another word for about five minutes while Laurie held forth on volleyball.

"Still," said Marilee when Laurie finally paused for breath, "in water polo we have all that and have to swim besides."

"But field hockey!" protested Irma. "The complications! You have to think of everything at once. . . ."

They all sighed deeply, each trying to outsigh the others by way of indicating that her sport was the hardest.

And of course they still had to contend with the school bus comedians.

"Hey, Sammy, did you hear about the funny thing that happened last Friday?"

"No, Gino, what was it?"

"A hockey game! Talk about laughs, we should have been there!"

"Gino," said Irma in scathing tones, "why don't you get your own TV show?"

"My agent's working on it," said Gino, fingering an imaginary cigar. "When I get it going, I'll give you hockey girls a guest shot. We can always use some good slapstick."

"We'll give you some with our hockey sticks!"

"Oh, gee, Sammy, she's done it again! She's hurt my feelings. I think I'm gonna cry," wailed Gino, and sobbed noisily on Sammy's shoulder.

At home Irma had to put up with further comedy turns, this time of the heavy-handed parental variety.

"Well, how's the lady hockey star tonight? This ought to save me a lot of money. Before you're through I expect you'll be getting some nice athletic scholarship offers from the colleges."

"Dear Abby," mused Irma, "should a girl tell her own father to drop dead? . . ."

"She's got another bad bruise on her shin from one of those clubs," said her mother. "I'm not sure I approve of—"

"Sticks, Mom, not clubs. Anyway, it's nothing," said Irma, who was rather proud of having taken a few knocks without complaining. After nearly every scrimmage there was a general post mortem comparison of bruises and a tendency to swagger a little if you had a good one.

"If you ask me, I think she's beginning to like the game," said her father, but of course Irma could not let a statement like that go unchallenged.

"Oh, it's all right, but it's rotten hard work," she said. "Don't think it won't be heavenly when our trial program is over and we don't have to go out there and slave away at practice, practice, practice three times a week. It's a trial, all right! I don't get anything else done!"

"That's true," her mother agreed. "It *will* be nice when you have more free time and I can get a little work out of you around here."

"Aw, Mom!"

One afternoon over on Fillmore Street Irma saw Doctor Ben's car parked in front of old Mrs. Minerva Biggerstaff's. At that moment he came out of the house carrying his little black bag. She stopped her bike beside his car and waited for him.

"How's Aunt Min today?" That was what everyone in the village called her, whether they were related to her or not.

"She's enjoying her usual poor health," he reported.

"How about Miss Tingley?"

"Need I say? For a woman her age, it's remarkable."

"It's all that fresh air she's getting, sitting at the window."

"Ha ha."

"I'm glad she's doing so well, anyway. Does that mean that after all she may be able to—"

"No! If there's any silly rumor going around to that effect you can forget it!"

"There's no rumor I know of," said Irma primly, "unless of course I decide to start one."

"Well, don't, or by heaven I'll set my snakes on you!"

11

At the end of their final practice before the game, Miss Tingley had a few words to say to them. Bundled up in a big parka that made her look tinier than ever, she sat at the window and gazed down at them with bright, serious eyes.

"Well, girls, I think you're ready. You're ready to give a good account of yourselves. But let us not deceive ourselves, it will be a stern test. You will be playing confident opponents on an unfamiliar field. It makes one think of the ancient Greeks, far from home on the windy plains of Troy. But you will be as stouthearted as they, and we will have our heroes, too. Do your best, give it all you have, and show Hyde Park they have something quite different to contend with this time!"

When they boarded the bus that was to take them to the game they were excited, laughing and chattering. Before long, however, the laughter and the chatter died away. They grew subdued and thoughtful. Glancing around her, Irma knew they were all thinking the same things. They were wishing they could have gotten that first terrible game out of the way on Hyde Park's field and been able to play this one on their own ground. For one thing, then Miss Tingley would have been able to watch and help—just knowing her fiery eye was on them would have helped! As it was, Hyde Park seemed to have every advantage.

When they arrived they found the whole Hyde Park squad warming up on the field. Irma's heart sank. It looked like an army.

> The Assyrian came down like the wolf
> on the fold
> And his cohorts were gleaming
> in purple and gold. . .

One of Miss Tingley's favorite bits of poetry. Then Irma cheered up a bit, remembering that in the poem the Assyrian didn't make out so well, after all. And how about David and Goliath? Her spirits sagged again. Judging from pictures Miss Tingley had shown them, David might have been small but was impressively muscular. Did they have enough muscle for the job?

Backed by Lally Beecham and one or two other players, Hyde Park's coach, Mrs. Carmichael, welcomed them. The girls looked smug, bored, and supremely confident. Maybe even—Irma welcomed the thought with a little lift of excitement—maybe even overconfident. The way Goliath must have looked when he lumbered forward and saw the little squirt who had had the audacity to challenge him.

"Why don't you take ten minutes to warm up and then we'll start the game?" suggested Mrs. Carmichael, and Mrs. Draper said that would be just fine.

While they were arming themselves with their hockey sticks and getting ready to take the field, Irma circulated busily among her teammates, speaking with the cunning of Ulysses.

"Listen, let's not show off, let's try to look like we haven't improved much. Let them think they're going to walk all over us again," she muttered, being careful not to let Mrs. Draper hear her.

Fran, tense and earnest, gave her a startled glance, automatically disapproving—but then her eyes widened with sudden understanding and she actually grinned.

"Right!" she cried in a low voice. "We'll psych

them! If we can just get them off on the wrong foot. . . . It might work!"

The word was passed with classroom efficiency. When they began to dribble and pass, nothing like precision was anywhere evident. And good old Drape reacted perfectly, hovering around with a distressed expression that made her look like the Droopy of old.

"Girls! Settle down, watch what you're doing, don't be nervous!"

Glancing down the field out of the corner of her eye, Irma saw that Lally and her teammates were not missing anything. She saw eyes roll toward the Wagstaff squad, saw grins exchanged, and heard Lally's silvery laugh tinkle on the breeze.

For once Lally's laugh was music to her ears.

The ball was centered at midfield, the center forwards were squared off for the first bully.

Tap, clash—tap, clash—tap, clash—and Fran feinted beautifully. She lifted the blade of her stick and Hyde Park's center forward hit the ball under it at the wrong angle, straight to her opponents' right inner. Irma and Fran pulled off a triangular pass, leaving the center forward behind, and Irma pushed a diagonal pass to Angie at left inner the instant she had fielded Fran's return.

Overconfidence was indeed the word. Hyde Park's forward line was caught flat-footed, and Lally Beecham at center half had a sudden look of alarm on her face as she called out to her back-field and charged in to tackle. But Angie, swinging around the ball like a crab, had already lined a difficult square pass to the right which Fran picked up on the run near the striking circle. She looked all ready to pass to her left, but instead pushed the ball to the right again into the striking circle, where Linda at right wing flashed in on a sharp angle and flicked the ball past the goalie into the far corner of the cage.

The Wagstaff team reacted like eleven Mexican jumping beans. One play, and they had taken the lead! Come what may, they had scored first! Over on the sideline the rest of their squad were screaming and hugging each other, and poor Drape was looking absolutely bewildered, but happy.

Irma did her share of the cheering, but she had no illusions as to their chances of reversing the situation and walking all over Hyde Park this time. Once that team settled down and started to function, it would be another story. There was a lot of game left to play. But at least this time there would be none of that 11 to 0 stuff! No matter what happened now, the final score would at least be Something to—1!

Annoyed with themselves, Hyde Park lined up for the center bully that started play again after a score, and from then on were no longer an over-confident team that could be caught napping.

Nevertheless, they were shaken up, and had trouble hitting their stride. As with any team that had been caught off balance, it took them a while to find themselves. For an amazingly long time play was hot and heavy, but with neither team scoring again. That single goal began to look better and better. Irma almost began to hope—

But then Nan Pratt fouled a Hyde Park player inside Wagstaff's striking circle, which gave Hyde Park a penalty corner hit.

The hit was taken from the goal line at a point ten yards from the cage. For a penalty corner hit, the defending backs had to line up behind the goal line and stay there until the ball had been hit. The offensive line ringed the striking circle just outside the line. The instant the ball was struck the defensive backs could rush into the circle to mark the attackers or intercept the ball.

Hyde Park's left wing drove the ball perfectly to her left inner in the striking circle. Eager to redeem her error, Nan sprang forward to tackle, and committed another error. She unsighted the goalie, Bunky—blocked her line of vision—and the ball got past both of them. It was not poor Nan's day.

Being scored on was a depressing experience. It pricked the beautiful, iridescent soap bubble of hope that had been floating around in the mind of every Wagstaff player—a vision of 1 to 0—and the result was unfortunate. Some of the wind was knocked out of the Wagstaff team.

Their play sagged a little, only a little, but enough to open up the game for Hyde Park, to give them a chance to make spaces for passes, to get away from defenders who were not marking closely enough, to battle their way three times into the striking circle. Twice Bunky stopped shots for goal with her feet and cleared the ball to the side. The third time Lally Beecham, of all people, came in from nowhere to drive home Hyde Park's second score.

Lally was surrounded by her capering teammates as both teams turned back toward midfield to take positions for a center bully. Now they had taken the lead, now they had regained their rightful place. Half-trudging, half-trotting along behind them, the Wagstaff girls called out encouragement to one another and tried to hide their disappointment. Reaching midfield, they began to line up.

And it was then that Irma, glancing dejectedly toward her team's bench, saw a sight she would never forget. No girl on the field that day was destined ever to forget it.

Slowly, slowly toward the Wagstaff bench came an outlandish procession. Almost lost in her parka, with her leg in its cast stretched out on its platform ahead of her, Miss Tingley sat very straight in her wheelchair. Carefully easing it over the rough turf were two boys who had either volunteered or been commandeered. Gino

Minelli and Sammy Arbuckle! Beside the chair walked Doctor Ben Fulton. He had the worn look of a man who had recently lost an argument.

"Look!" squealed Irma. "It's Miss Tingley!"

Hyde Park's captain was still nearby, having stopped to speak to her forwards. Hearing Irma's outburst, she turned and said, "Wha-a-a-t?" as though not sure she had heard correctly.

Irma was so astonished and excited she blurted out an explanation without thinking.

"Miss Tingley! She's our coach!"

Lally took a look, and this time her reaction had no silvery tinkle to it. This time it was a plain horse laugh. "Oh, my gosh! That old mummy? Well, this explains everything!" She put her head on one side and simpered in a sweetie-pie voice, "Goodness, doesn't she just make you feel *tingly* all over?"

She had no more than spoken when the horn blew. The first half was over. Bubbling with girlish laughter, Lally turned and rushed off the field, calling to her teammates, "Hey, kids, wait till you hear this! You're not going to believe it!"

For a moment Irma was transfixed, paralyzed by sheer rage. She had never been angrier in her life. And when she turned and saw Fran Sealey's face, she knew she had company.

"Did you hear that, Fran?"

"Yes!"

"I'm glad we can stop. I'm so mad I couldn't play!"

"Me, too. That stinker!"

Seething with anger, they ran toward the sideline. And afterwards they could not remember who said it first as they ran, because they both thought of it at the same instant—

"Listen, let's pass the word around!"

"Right! Let them all know what she said—"

"And what they're laughing about over there!"

"But not in front of—"

"Of course not!"

By the time they reached the sideline, Miss Tingley had disappeared from sight, surrounded by her squad. They pushed in for a glimpse of her. She had Mrs. Draper by the hand, and she was beaming.

"Splendid, girls, splendid! So you scored first, and have held the score to only two to one at half time! You are doing just what I knew you would do, you are giving a good account of yourselves. But I simply couldn't bear to miss the entire game. Of course, at *first* dear Doctor Fulton would not hear of it—"

Dear Doctor Fulton made a sort of animal sound in his throat and looked as if he were about to choke to death, but Miss Tingley blithely continued.

"—and I had great difficulty persuading him I was perfectly fit to come, but at last he saw the light—though not without causing me to miss the entire first half, I am sorry to find," she added with a reproving glance that brought forth further strangling sounds from her personal physician. "But now, let's see you girls acquit yourselves in the second half as brilliantly as you have in the first and bring our brief season to a fitting conclusion!"

Loud cheering ensued. When it had subsided, Fran Sealey got in a word.

"Miss Tingley, may we go into a huddle to talk things over before the second half starts?"

"By all means, Fran. Go sit down on the field and make your plans. Unless Mrs. Draper wants to add something, that is. I have nothing further to say."

The Drape's flustered glance swept around the circle.

"No, I don't think. . . . Well, except that I'd like to know what went on in that pregame warm-up—but still, that can keep till later. . . ."

Fran raised an imperious hand.

"Okay, then, let's go. Everybody!"

She glanced at Irma and jerked her head, and together they led the way onto the field. When everyone was in a circle, Fran surprised Irma with a bit of what could only be called teamwork.

"Okay, Irma. You tell them what you said, and tell them what *she* said."

They were trotting to their places for the beginning of the second half. Irma's eyes strayed toward the side of the field and she noticed a couple of persons she had almost forgotten about. Gino and Sammy had posted themselves on the sideline. Gino raised his hands together above his head in a boxer's salute.

"Go get 'em, champ!"

Irma brandished her hockey stick at the boys, fierce as an Amazon, and bared her teeth. In her present frame of mind she could take anything, even Gino and Sammy.

The center forwards squared off, the whistle blew, and the second half began.

12 _____

The Wagstaff team was playing with a sort of controlled fury now, and the important ingredient was control. Hotheaded anger could have been disastrous, with ragged play the result; but they had gone beyond that.

Hyde Park played well, but Wagstaff's stubborn backfield broke up every attack, while their forward line threatened again and again until a permanent scared look settled on the face of the Hyde Park goalie. But neither side scored, and the precious minutes dwindled away.

Then all at once there was a wild scramble in

the Hyde Park striking circle. The ball was a blur at Irma's feet as she charged in. Somehow she got her stick on it, somehow she scooped, and neither the hands nor the feet of the goalie were quick enough. The ball bounced sweetly against the back of the net.

She had made her first score in a game, and it was the most delirious experience she could remember. Teammates hugged her and screamed in her ears, her legs felt numb, her face was afire, and all she could think of was, If only we can hold them now for just a few more minutes!

But then play had hardly started again when Nan Pratt took a spill. When she got up she was limping. It was definitely not Nan's day. Still insisting she would be all right, she was helped to the sidelines. Play was suspended while they waited for the substitute right half. Sally, maybe, or possibly Maureen. . . .

"Good grief! Is that. . . ?"

"Has Miss Tingley lost her marbles?"

Dodie Fenwick was loping into the game.

It was true, of course, that Dodie had been switched to right half on the second team—but at a time like this, to send her into a real game! Shaken to the core, ten other Wagstaff girls made a desperate resolve to do a little more than their best in order to plug the hole in their lineup.

They got a surprise.

Miss Tingley seemed to know what she was

doing. It was true, as she had observed, that Dodie had long legs, and today Dodie used them.

It was Dodie who covered the way a wing half should, who raced back and forth without letup, and who tackled Hyde Park's left wing so gamely she spoiled what looked like a sure shot at goal.

And then it was Dodie, with hardly a minute to go, who took a push-in from around the Wagstaff twenty-five-yard line.

The ball had been driven over the sideline by a Hyde Park player. In such cases a player from the other team pushed or flicked the ball back onto the field from the point at which it went out. It was important to take push-ins quickly, because putting the ball briskly into play again gave opponents that much less time to get into position to mark and cover properly.

To be quick was one thing, but Dodie's movements this time were something extra. The instant the ball crossed the sideline she pounced on it like a cat. Nobody had ever seen Dodie move so fast in all her life. Furthermore, she managed to look as if she were going to send the ball out to Mary Margolis at center half—but instead pushed it straight up the sideline to her right wing, Linda Katz, who was charging back down the line and was wide open.

Linda fielded the ball and seemed to change

position in midair as she drove a diagonal pass to Irma. And Irma, racing to pick up the pass, was well ahead of the field, with Hyde Park's defense dangerously thin ahead of her. Only one player and the goalie stood between her and the cage, with a third player diagonaling across the field trying to overtake her. No one on her own team had caught up with her as yet to give her a chance to pass.

Crab apples.

Three crab apples were ahead of her, and all she had to do was maneuver the crab apple she was dribbling around them.

A dodge worked on the first player—a push to her non-stick side followed up by a swerve around her to pick up the ball again.

The player overtaking her angled in and tried a circular tackle. A scoop at the last instant took care of that one, with the ball just clearing the defender's blade, and then Irma was charging at an angle toward the striking circle, and the goalie was coming out to meet her, straight at her, trying to spoil her line of vision. The striking circle and clouds of glory were straight ahead, because somehow she was going to get a shot past that goalie.

"Irma!"

It was Fran's voice, and Fran flickered there in the corner of her left eye, with Lally Beecham right on her heels. Everything in Irma's mind, heart, and soul yearned to shoot for goal, but her reflexes did the right thing. She pushed a short pass straight in front of Fran, and Fran did not miss.

Everyone on the Wagstaff team came running, even the goalie, and while they were still in one big excited muddle the horn blasted and the game was over, and then all the players on the bench erupted onto the field, too. A four-letter word fouled the atmosphere near Irma. She turned and saw it had come from Lally Beecham. She gave Lally a sweet smile.

"Doesn't it just make you feel tingly all over?" she asked, and left Lally to think it over.

Ahead of her Fran had been lifted onto shoulders, but she was twisting and pointing. The ones who responded, however, were not her teammates. It was a jubilant pair of boys who raced out to meet Irma.

"Yowie! I thought you were going to blow it, Irma, but you didn't! You made the team play!" cried Gino in a hoarse voice that sounded as if he had been doing some cheering himself. The next thing she knew she was a passenger on the last pair of shoulders in the world she had ever expected to ride anywhere on.

What's more, she was liking it.

Mrs. Carmichael came marching over for a brief moment and won vast respect in the Wagstaff camp.

"Congratulations, Miss Tingley," she said, shaking hands. "Your girls gave our girls exactly what they've been needing."

"We were lucky, Mrs. Carmichael," said Miss Tingley, magnanimous in victory. She glanced around and seemed genuinely puzzled. "Really, I don't know what got into them!"

Her physician was busy mopping his ruddy brow. His own sideline gymnastics and vocal efforts had not been trifling. Irma cocked a pleased eye at him.

"Well, what did you think of that, Doctor Ben?"

He glowered sideways at his patient.

"That woman!" he said, and shook his head. But then he made an honest admission. "Still, I wouldn't have missed it!"

Dodie seemed to agree. Her hair was stringy, her face was flushed, and the hands she held up were well smudged with the grime of the battlefield. She held them up, fingers spread wide.

"I haven't got a fingernail left!" she cried, "but it was worth it!"

The Saturday after their game it snowed. Winter had announced itself. Walking home from Marilee's, Irma stopped to look at Old Faithful. There it was, leaning against its tree as always, with a cap of snow on its head. Crunching over through gathering drifts, she took the stick from its place and held it up for a critical look.

"You!" she said. "Just think what you got me into!"

Then she put Old Faithful on her shoulder and took it home and hung it on the wall over her table.